The Secret of the Stones

A FOLKTALE

retold by **Robert D. San Souci**

pictures by **James Ransome**

PHYLLIS FOGELMAN BOOKS

NEW YORK

For Karen Judd
with happy memories of Oscar Parties, Hunan cuisine,
the Joffrey, and best of all, your continuing friendship!
—R.S.S.

To friends Barbara and James Carney
—J.R.

Published by Phyllis Fogelman Books
An imprint of Penguin Putnam Books for Young Readers
345 Hudson Street
New York, New York 10014

Text copyright © 2000 by Robert D. San Souci
Pictures copyright © 2000 by James Ransome
All rights reserved
Designed by Debora Smith and Atha Tehon
Printed in Hong Kong on acid-free paper
First Edition
3 5 7 9 10 8 6 4 2

Library of Congress Cataloging in Publication Data
San Souci, Robert D.
The secret of the stones: a folktale / retold by Robert D. San Souci;
pictures by James Ransome.—1st ed.
p.   cm.
Summary: When they try to find out who is doing their chores
while they are working in the fields, a childless couple discovers that
the two stones they have brought home are actually two bewitched orphans.
ISBN 0-8037-1640-0
[1. Afro-Americans—Folklore. 2. Folklore—United States.]
I. Ransome, James. II. Title.
PZ8.1.S227Se   2000   398.2
[E]—DC20   93-43952   CIP   AC

The illustrations were done in oils on paper.

*B*ack in the olden times there was a man and wife who had no children. John and Clara loved each other deeply, and labored together from sunup to dusk-dark. They hoed long rows of cotton; picked the ripened cotton; and tended a vegetable patch between times. Each night they ate a simple meal of peas, okra, beans, and corn bread, then fell wearily into bed.

Their cabin was a long way from their fields. One evening as they walked home along the creek that ran past their cabin east into the blue hills, Clara leaned down and picked up two little white stones lying side by side. They shone as pale and round and smooth as twin moons in her cinnamon-colored palm.

John asked, "What yo' gonna do with dose li'l rocks?"

"I'm gonna use 'em to sharpen our knives," Clara said.

At home she set them on the floor near the front door.

John built a cook-fire, and Clara fixed supper. They were so tired, neither of them gave another thought to the two stones.

When they got back from the cotton fields the next night, to their great surprise they found that someone had ironed their clothes, sawed the wood, and swept the cabin and porch. The same visitor had pounded the corn for their bread, drawn water from the creek, and had a fire made and everything set out to cook supper.

They looked all over, but couldn't find even a footprint.

"Who was it done de work?" John wondered.

"It a mystery, for sure," Clara agreed, shaking her head.

After their meal, while John washed the dishes, Clara sat at the table, using the white stones to whet her kitchen knives. Just a touch from the stones produced a gleaming, razor-sharp edge. When the couple blew out the lantern and climbed into bed, they saw the sharpened blades shining in the dark with a pale light, just as the stones did.

Each evening after that John and Clara found that someone had done the housework and yard work, then had gone away without a trace. Sometimes they ran home at midday, but they never saw anyone. They found corn partly ground or peas half-shelled or the broom on the floor, as if someone had stopped sweeping only a moment before.

They returned to the cotton fields in puzzlement. When they came back at day's end, the work was all finished.

One night as they sat on the porch, they saw a sturdy, strong-featured woman approaching. She was dressed in a black skirt with a pale blue blouse, and gold earrings that shone in the moonlight. People in the neighborhood called her "Aunt Easter," though she had no real kinfolk. Everyone was a little bit afraid of the woman, because she could see "hants" and knew healing secrets and could work charms and sometimes had "prophesyin'" dreams.

"Evenin', Aunt Easter," John and Clara called politely.

"I had a dream last night," the woman said. "It tol' me to tell yo' dat dose two li'l rocks yo' picked up isn't rocks. When yo' go to de field, dey turn inter an orphan boy an' girl an' do all yo' work. Den dey turn back inter rocks."

"Oh!" cried Clara, "I knew dose stones was special!"

John asked, "Is dere a way to see dem li'l chillen?"

Aunt Easter nodded. "Tomorrow, 'fore sunup, splash clean water on de floor an' throw some meal on it. Den hide, but don't make no sound." Then the woman went on her way.

Before the rooster crowed the next morning, John and Clara got up and sprinkled the floor with water and cornmeal. Then they hid behind the bed.

When the first light of dawn crept past the curtains, the stones suddenly grew into a boy and girl. They were barefoot and raggedy, but beautiful. They fairly flew around the cabin, working. First the boy sang:

Tubin, Tubidi!
Mister don't know
Dat de li'l stones
Chop de wood an' wash de clothes.
Telanga!

Then his sister sang:

Tubidi, Tubin!
Missus don't know
Dat de li'l stones
Grin' corn an' sweep de floh.
Telanga!

Clara, in hiding, felt her heart go out to the children. She wanted to kiss and hug them as if they were her very own boy and girl. She almost said something, when John whispered, "Aunt Easter said don't make a soun'."

But the girl swept so hard under the bed that she raised a fierce cloud of dust. John coughed and Clara sneezed.

Instantly the children vanished. There were only the two white stones beside the door.

"Oh," cried Clara, "I got to find a way to catch dem when dey is li'l chillen an' keep dem and raise dem like our own."

"Only way to do dat is to ask Aunt Easter fo' a charm," said John.

Clara agreed. So they filled a basket with snap beans and sweet potatoes for the woman. Then they followed the creek to Aunt Easter's cabin.

Aunt Easter was sitting on the front steps of her itty-bitty cabin. She thanked the couple for the food, then said, "I knew yo' was comin' 'cause I dreamed it. An' dat dream showed me where dose white stones come from.

"Dose chillen lived with dey ma an' pa on a farm up de mountain. But a conjure-man put a spell on dere folks, so dey sicken an' die. Den he go an' say he gonna care for dose orphans, but he work 'em almost to death. When dey run away, he turn 'em inter stones by de river. A flood carry dem to where yo' foun' dem.

"If yo' want to change dem back inter real chillen, yo' gotta fetch me three things from dat ole conjure-man."

"What things?" asked Clara.

"Milk from his white cow dat ain't got one black hair. Eggs from his white chickens dat ain't got a black feather. Corn dat ain't got one dark grain mixed in. Bring me dese, an' I can make a charm to bring dem chillen back for you."

"Tell us how to fine dat conjure-man," John said bravely.

"Just follow de creek to its end," said Aunt Easter.

Soon John and Clara set off hand in hand, following the creek into the blue mountains. The path grew stonier and steeper, but they climbed onward. John carried a pail and Clara carried a basket.

At evening they found the place where the stream rose up from the ground. Nearby was a cabin. Behind it was a cowshed with a single pure white cow and a henhouse with a flock of pure white chickens. All around were cornfields, but every ear had been picked. "Dat corn must be stored in de house," whispered John.

"Look!" Clara whispered back. "Dere's de ole man!"

She pointed to a lamplit window, where the tall, thin conjure-man sat. His eyes were two narrow slits that made him look mean as a rattlesnake.

"He'll spell us bad if he catch us takin' his milk an' eggs an' corn," said John.

"Dose belong to de orphans," said Clara. "Now, I'm gonna go up to de door an' get him to let me in dere. While I talk with him, yo' fetch a pail o' milk and put some eggs in yo' shirt. Den yo' run into de wood an' make plenty o' noise. When he go out to see what's what, I'm gonna take some corn an' run off de other way. We can meet up later on de way home."

"Soun' like a good plan, but yo' be careful," said John, giving her a kiss.

When the old man answered her knock, Clara, carrying her empty basket, said politely, "How de do."

"What yo' want?" asked the old man gruffly. His snakey eyes and poisonous look made him seem more dangerous than a rattler—made him appear like the very devil himself.

But Clara summoned up all her courage and said, "I hear dat yo' can make me a charm to bring me good luck. I can pay." She patted the empty pocket of her skirt as if it held money.

"Come in, set down," said the conjure-man.

Clara shivered when she saw the jars and bottles and bowls that lined the shelves and the ledge above the blazing fireplace. These held spiders and powders and liquids and dried herbs and all sorts of unpleasant things.

In one corner she saw bushel baskets heaped with white corn. She sat down at a table, facing the man.

Suddenly they heard John shouting outside. Instantly the conjure-man yanked open the door, pulled from his pocket a wax bead with a hair wrapped around it, set it in his palm, and muttered a few words. Instantly the bead flew off into the dark. A moment later John cried out, then was silent.

Clara shrieked her husband's name. The conjure-man spun around and said, "So yo' was part o' dis mischief too. I fix yo' when I bring back what my witchball brung down."

He slammed the cabin door behind him. Clara couldn't pry the door or any window open. When she tried to break the glass, it just stretched like India rubber.

Then she remembered hearing once that a conjure-man's power rested in a conjure-bone, which he always kept in a secret place. She frantically searched the cabin for it; just as she was about to give up, she found a yellowed bone like the backbone of a large rat, hidden beneath a loose hearthstone.

Clara snatched up the bone just as the conjure-man returned, dragging the unconscious John behind him. When he saw what she was holding, he cried, "Put dat down, or I—"

But Clara flung the bone into the fire. The conjure-man began to roll around, shrieking, "Yo' burnin' me!"

The fire blazed up; the conjure-man shrank down to an ugly black bug.

"Dis for all de misery yo' caused dem chillen," Clara said, squashing the bug. It popped with a stink of burned sulfur.

At that moment John woke up. "I spill de milk an' broke de eggs," he said unhappily.

"Don't matter," said Clara, embracing him. "Dere ain't no one to stop us takin' all de eggs an' milk we need, now."

They stayed the night in the cabin. At daybreak they hurried to Aunt Easter's cabin. Straightaway the woman ground the corn, mixed it with the milk and eggs, added salt and flour and some other things.

"She just makin' corn bread," John said softly.

Clara nodded, her heart sinking as she watched the other woman pour the batter into two tin breadpans and set them in the heated oven. All three sat silently while the cabin filled with the aroma of baking bread.

When Aunt Easter pulled out the two golden loaves of corn bread, she said, "Tomorrow sprinkle water an' meal like before. Put dis corn bread on de table, den hide. When de chillen eat de bread, yo' say dese words." And she told them words to break the spell.

At dawn John sprinkled water and Clara scattered meal. Then they put the corn bread on the table and hid behind the bed.

When the stones turned into the boy and girl, the children stared at the corn bread, then each began eating.

John stood up behind the bed and said:

Tubin, Tubidi!
Daddy say,
"Feed de li'l chillen
So dey won't go away."
Telanga!

The children expected to turn back into stones. When this did not happen, they clung to one another and began to cry.

But Clara came out from behind the bed and said gently:

Tubidi, Tubin!
Mammy say,
"Kiss de chillen's foreheads
So dey will always stay."
Telanga!

She did just that. Then Clara and John hugged the children, turning their tears to smiles. They called their new son "Tubin" and their new daughter "Tubidi." And the children lived happily ever after with their new Pa and Ma.

Telanga!

About the Story

The folktale on which this retelling is based comes from several sources. A brief version was printed in Fred W. Allsopp's *Folklore of Romantic Arkansas,* Volume II (New York: The Grolier Society, 1931) as "Tubin, Tubidi—The Two Little Stones." A variant of the tale, called "The Two White Stones," was published in Virginia Holladay's *Bantu Tales* (New York: The Viking Press, 1970). Mrs. Holladay founded and taught at the Central School for missionary children in the Congo (now the Democratic Republic of the Congo) from 1927 until 1940. She collected stories from her pupils, who were Baluba (now Luba) and Lulua people from the Kasai district.

The story in the Arkansas collection was printed roughly at the same time Holladay was doing her field work. Such details as the childless couple, the two white stones, the meeting with a wise woman, and the need for a white goat, a white chicken, and cornmeal to break the spell on the children are identical in both renditions. This suggests that the American version is a remarkably unchanged survival of an African root story. For narrative purposes, I have changed the "white goat" to a "white cow" in my retelling.

The poetry is adapted from some brief lines in the Arkansas version. The expanded narrative, I hope, remains true in particulars and in spirit to its African and African-American roots.

—R.S.S.